LEVEL 5

Re-told by: Paul Shipton
Series Editor: Melanie Williams

Pearson Education Limited
Edinburgh Gate, Harlow,
Essex CM20 2JE, England
and Associated Companies throughout the world.

ISBN: 978-1-4082-8872-6

This edition first published by Pearson Education Ltd 2012

9 10

Set in 15/19pt OT Fiendstar
Printed in China
SWTC/09

Acknowledgements
The publisher would like to thank the following for their kind permission to reproduce their photographs:
(Key: b-bottom; c-centre; l-left; r-right; t-top)
Fotolia.com: auremar 31 (f), Nikolai Sorokin 31 (d), Studio Barcelona 31 (e);
Shutterstock.com: Denise Kappa 31 (g), Nejron Photo 31 (h)

Every effort has been made to trace the copyright holders and we apologise in
advance for any unintentional omissions. We would be pleased to insert the appropriate
acknowledgement in any subsequent edition of this publication.

Published by Pearson Education Ltd.

For a complete list of the titles available in the Pearson English Kids Readers series, please go to
www.pearsonenglishkidsreaders.com. Alternatively, write to your local Pearson Education office or to
Pearson English Readers Marketing Department, Pearson Education, Edinburgh Gate, Harlow, Essex CM202JE, England.

Remy was very different from all the other rats. They were happy to eat old food, garbage ... *anything*.

But Remy loved food. He loved to smell and taste new things to eat. He loved to eat and soon he loved to cook, too.

"You have talent," his brother Emile told him.

His father Django just said, "Eat your garbage."

Remy did not listen. Sometimes he went up into the kitchen at night and read the cookery books there.

One night, the woman of the house woke up and saw Remy in the kitchen.

"Ahhh!" she cried.

Django heard this from under the floor. "Run to the boats!" he shouted.

Humans hated rats – it was time to leave!

All of the rats ran outside and jumped into the boats.

Remy ran too, but it was not easy with his favorite cookery book in his little paws.

"Quickly, Son!" shouted Django. The water carried the boats into the sewer.

The cookery book was Remy's boat.

He tried to follow the others, but he lost them in the fast waters of the sewer.

The water carried him along for hours. At last, his boat stopped. With no family or friends, Remy sat and read the book. There was a picture of a man on the front. His name was Gusteau and he was a famous old chef.

"A good chef must not be afraid to try new things," the book said.

Remy wanted to try new things so he decided to leave the sewer. He climbed up into the building above.

It was full of humans, but Remy was careful. He climbed higher and higher, up to the roof. From there he could see the whole city at night.

"It's Paris!" Remy said in surprise. "And it's *beautiful*!"

There was a big sign on the building opposite him.

It was Gusteau's restaurant. He was the chef who wrote the cookery book!

Remy looked down through the window into the kitchen and watched the chefs at work.

Not all the people there were chefs. It was the job of one tall boy to take out the garbage. He was near a pot of soup when his arm hit it. Some of the soup fell out. The boy looked around quickly. Then he started to put water and new ingredients in the pot.

"No!" cried Remy. "That soup will be terrible!"

When Remy shouted, he fell through the window and down into the kitchen.

A busy kitchen in a restaurant was a dangerous place for a rat! Remy ran for the window quickly, before any chefs saw him.

He stopped when he was near the soup. He could smell it.

Salt! That soup did not have enough salt! Or pepper ... or spices.

Remy forgot about the danger and started to cook.

The tall boy returned. His mouth opened in surprise when he saw Remy cooking. Suddenly, an angry voice shouted,

"What are you doing?"

This was Chef Skinner. After Gusteau died, the restaurant became Skinner's.

Skinner did not see Remy. "Garbage boys cannot cook in *my* kitchen!" he shouted at the tall boy. "This is your last night here, Linguini! Now throw this soup away!"

One of the chefs said, "A waiter already took some of that soup to a customer."

When the waiter returned, Skinner waited for the bad news –
did the customer hate the soup? No!

"She LOVES it," said the waiter. "And she isn't just a customer.
She's a restaurant *critic*!"

Colette, the only woman chef at Gusteau's, said, "Linguini can't
lose his job now!"

Skinner tasted the soup. It was good – *delicious*! But did Linguini
really make it?

"You're going to make that soup again," he told Linguini.
"And *I'm* going to watch you!"

Remy did not want to stay in the kitchen. He was nearly at the window when Skinner saw him.

"Rat!" cried the chef angrily. "GET IT!"

All of the chefs moved fast. Remy tried to run, but Linguini dropped a jar over him. He put the top on the jar quickly.

"What shall I do with it?" he asked.

"Take it far away from here!" shouted Skinner.

Linguini ran outside and rode his bicycle quickly to the river.

Linguini could not throw the little rat into the river.

"What did you put in that soup anyway? Spices?" he cried. "Wait! Did ... you just move your head?"

The rat's head moved again – yes.

"Can you *understand* me?" Linguini asked.

Again Remy's head moved – yes.

"I can't cook," Linguini said to the rat unhappily. "I'm only here because my mother was Gusteau's friend." Suddenly, Linguini had an idea. "I can't cook, but perhaps *you* can help me!"

Linguini took Remy back to his little apartment. But how could the rat help the human to cook?

Remy had the best idea. He sat on Linguini's head and held two pieces of hair. When Remy pulled the left piece of hair, Linguini's left hand moved. When he pulled the other piece, Linguini's right hand moved.

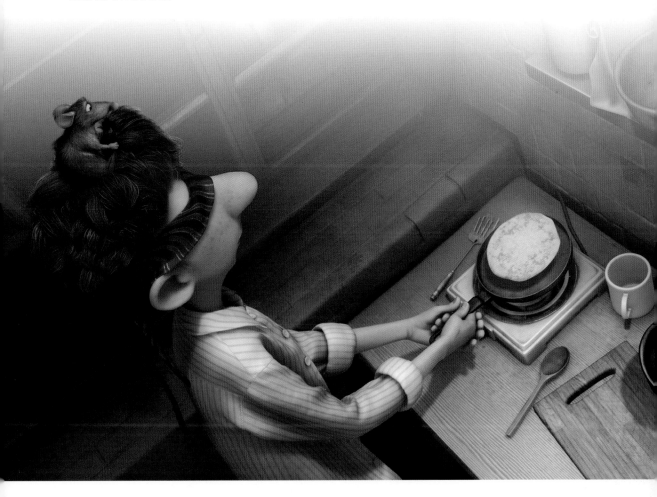

Then they just had to practice for hours and hours.

After a lot of practice, Remy could control Linguini's hands. Now he could cook!

Remy and Linguini were ready to go to Gusteau's restaurant and make the soup again for Chef Skinner.

In the kitchen of Gusteau's restaurant, Remy hid under Linguini's hat. He remembered the words of Chef Gusteau and controlled everything. With his help, Linguini made the soup again.

When the soup was ready, Skinner tasted it.

"It's good," he said unhappily. The little chef did not really want Linguini in his kitchen, but now he *had* to keep him.

Linguini made the same soup every day, with Remy's help, and the customers loved it. But one day ...

"One customer wants a *different* meal," said the waiter.

Skinner chose an old Gusteau recipe and told Linguini and Colette to make it.

"We *never* use that recipe," said one of the chefs. "Gusteau hated it!"

Skinner knew that. He *wanted* the meal to be terrible. Then he could send Linguini away from his kitchen.

Colette and Linguini started to cook.

"Remember," Colette said. "Always follow the recipe carefully."

But from under Linguini's hat, Remy looked at all the ingredients. This recipe was *terrible*! So he decided to change it.

Before the waiter took the meal to the customer, Colette looked at the food on the plate.

"That's not the recipe!" she cried.

But it was too late. The customer already had the meal.

Soon, the waiter returned. "The customer *loves* Linguini's recipe!" he said.

Remy was happy because the customer liked his new recipe. A lot of the other customers also wanted it.

After work, Remy went outside behind the restaurant.

Suddenly, he saw a dark shape at the garbage. There were two red eyes in the night. Remy was afraid, but then ...

"Remy!"

"Remy!" His brother Emile jumped into the light. Remy was very happy to see his little brother again.

"Come and see Dad and the other rats!" Emile cried.

Django was happy to see his older son again.

"Welcome home, Remy," he said.

"Dad, I … I don't want to stay," Remy said. "I like my new life in the restaurant."

Django was angry now. "You can't change humans!" he shouted. "They only want to kill rats!"

Remy remembered Gusteau's words. *A good chef must not be afraid to try new things.*

"Any person can change," he said quietly and he turned to leave.

Remy returned to the restaurant. The next day, he met Emile again.

"Will you get us some of that delicious restaurant food?" Emile asked.

Remy was not sure. "I can get you food, but one time only," he said.

He ran inside to Skinner's office. Where was the key for the little room with all the food?

The key was not in Skinner's desk, but Remy saw two letters there. One was from Chef Gusteau, before he died. The other was from Linguini's mother, Renata.

Remy read the letters. Renata was Gusteau's good friend. Gusteau wanted Renata's son to have his restaurant.

Remy looked up. Linguini was Renata's son! Linguini did not know it, but Gusteau's restaurant was *his*, not Skinner's!

Suddenly, the door opened. Skinner was there! But Remy was much faster than the chef. He ran out of the office with the two letters in his mouth.

He had to show the letters to Linguini.

As soon as Linguini saw those letters, his life changed. Chef Skinner had to leave quickly before the police caught him.

Now the restaurant was *Linguini's,* and he was the new star of the Paris restaurant world. All the newspapers wanted his photo for their front page. They all wanted to write stories about the great new food at Gusteau's restaurant. Linguini happily answered all their questions about cookery.

Remy just stayed under Linguini's hat and listened to everything.

Suddenly a tall, thin man came into the restaurant. All the people became quiet. This was Anton Ego. He was the most famous restaurant critic in Paris. Every chef in the city was afraid of him. Ego only ate the best food. When he did not like a restaurant, he wrote a bad review in the newspaper and the restaurant closed!

Ego looked at Linguini now. "Tomorrow night I will eat here at Gusteau's restaurant," he said.

Remy was not happy. People loved the restaurant now and Linguini was suddenly famous. But Linguini was not really the chef, *Remy* was! The rat wanted the world to know his secret.

Linguini felt bad. The food was only good because of Remy. The world could not know their secret. But Linguini was angry, too.

"You don't control everything in this kitchen!" he cried. "You're not the only chef with talent here!"

Remy left the kitchen angrily.

Outside the restaurant, Remy found his brother. More of Emile's friends were with him now, and they were all hungry.

"Can we have some more delicious food from your restaurant?" Emile asked his brother.

Remy was still angry with Linguini, so this time he did not stop to think. "You can have *a lot* of food from the restaurant today!" he told his brother and the other rats. "Go and tell all of the rats. We're going inside."

Remy led the rats into the restaurant kitchen and showed them the room with all the food.

Suddenly, there was the sound of feet – human feet. All of the rats hid just before Linguini turned on the light. Only Remy stayed out on the kitchen floor.

Linguini looked down at his little friend. "I'm really sorry," he said. "I didn't mean it. This place is nothing without you."

From a corner of the kitchen, Django heard everything that Linguini said.

Linguini went to the room with the food and turned on the light. There were rats everywhere.

"What's happening?" Linguini cried. He turned to Remy. "You're *stealing* food from the restaurant? *Go away*! Go away *now*!"

Hundreds of rats ran from the kitchen, and Remy ran with them.

Linguini looked at the empty kitchen. It was nearly time for Ego to arrive. He had to cook the most important meal in his life ... *without* Remy!

When the other chefs arrived, Linguini was very nervous.

He was more nervous when a waiter said, "Anton Ego is here!"

Linguini did not know what to do. He could not cook without Remy.

Suddenly, he saw something on the floor — Remy! His friend was back to help him!

Then another chef saw Remy! "Rat!" he shouted.

"Wait!" cried Linguini. He picked Remy up. "I have to tell you something. I didn't cook anything. This *rat* is really the chef!"

The chefs listened to Linguini and then they left. They did not want to work with a rat! Only Colette stayed to help. But they could not cook for Ego without all the chefs.

"I was wrong about your friend ... and about you." Django told his son. "If you really want to do this, all of the rats can help. We're not chefs but we can listen."

Soon hundreds of rats were in the kitchen.

The rats all did the jobs that Remy told them to do.

Colette watched Remy carefully. "You're making *ratatouille* for Anton Ego?" she asked. "But that's just vegetable stew!"

But Remy's ratatouille was different. When the waiter brought his meal, Ego just looked at it. *Ratatouille?*

Then he tasted some of the stew. It was the most delicious food in the world!

After dinner, Ego asked to see the chef, and Linguini brought Remy to the table.

Ego listened carefully.

The next day Ego wrote his review of the restaurant. "Years ago Gusteau said, 'Anyone can cook.' Now I understand these words. Not all people can cook well, but a great chef can come from *anywhere*. Yesterday, I ate the most delicious meal in my life. The chef was the strangest … and also the *best* in all of Paris."

Before You Read

❶ Match the words and pictures. You can use a dictionary.

> waiter   recipe   spice   customer
> jar   cookery book   pot   chef

❷ This book is called Ratatouille. What do you think ratatouille is?

Activity page ❷

After You Read

❶ Circle the correct answer.

1 Remy lost his friends and family in ...
- **a** the house
- **b** the sewer
- **c** the restaurant

2 Remy controls Linguini with ...
- **a** the chef's hat
- **b** a cookery book
- **c** his hair

3 Linguini is ...
- **a** Renata's son
- **b** Chef Skinner's son
- **c** Colette's brother

4 Anton Ego writes ...
- **a** a new recipe
- **b** a cookery book
- **c** a review

❷ Finish the sentences with the right phrases.

1 Remy sees a sign for Gusteau's restaurant ...

2 Remy makes the soup ...

3 Remy teaches Linguini ...

4 Remy sees an important letter ...

- **a** on the roof.
- **b** in Skinner's office.
- **c** at Linguini's apartment.
- **d** in the restaurant kitchen.

❸ What do you think? Which of these sentences are NOT main ideas in the book?

1 It is good to try new things.

2 People can change.

3 Always stay with your family.

4 You can find talent in surprising places.